The Manhattan New School
311 E. 82nd Street
New York, New York 10028
(212) 734-7127

Text copyright © 1964 by Nord-Süd Verlag AG, Gossau Zürich, Switzerland
Illustrations copyright © 1991 by Nord Süd Verlag AG
First published in Switzerland under the title *Das Eichhorn und das Nashörnchen*
English translation copyright © 1991 by Nord-Süd Verlag AG

First published in the United States, Great Britain, Canada,
Australia, and New Zealand in 1991 by North-South Books,
an imprint of Nord-Süd Verlag AG.
First paperback edition published in 1998.

Library of Congress Cataloging-in-Publication Data is available.
A CIP catalogue record for this book is available from The British Library.

ISBN 1-55858-882-5
1 3 5 7 9 PB 10 8 6 4 2

Printed in Belgium

For more information about our books, and the authors and artists
who create them, visit our web site: http://www.northsouth.com

THE
Big Squirrel
AND THE
Little Rhinoceros

By Mischa Damjan
Illustrated by Hans de Beer

Translated by Lenny Hort

North-South Books
New York

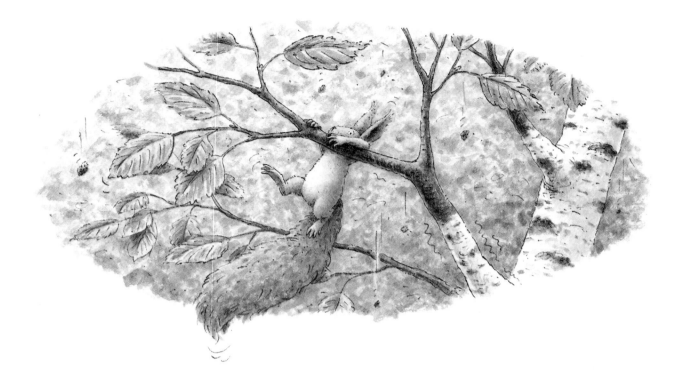

One morning as the sun rose over the Land of a
Thousand Shadows, the rhinoceros's head began to
itch. Since he couldn't scratch the itch with his big feet,
he charged straight at the first tree he saw. *Wham!*
The tree toppled over and a sleepy squirrel tumbled to
the ground. "Watch where you're going, you big oaf!"
the squirrel scolded. But the rhinoceros just laughed.
The itch was gone and that was all that mattered.

About the same time, the lion marched through the meadow roaring so loud that the earth shook. "I am the greatest! I am the strongest! I am the King of the Beasts!"

A mouse peeked out of her burrow and squeaked, "You scared the daylights out of me. The strong should help the weak. That's the best way to prove your strength."

But the lion just laughed and flicked sand in her face with the tuft of his tail.

Later that day a crocodile started grinding and gnashing his teeth very loudly. A frog sitting on a nearby leaf croaked, "Stop it! How can I catch any flies when you're making that racket?"

But the crocodile just laughed, and gnashed his teeth more loudly than ever.

That night the squirrel, the mouse, and the frog called a meeting of all the little animals in the Land of a Thousand Shadows.

First the squirrel chattered, "I want to be big, so I can get even with the rhinoceros."

Then the mouse squeaked, "I want to be big, so I can get even with the lion."

Then the frog croaked, "I want to be big, so I can get even with the crocodile."

But the other animals were happy being small. One by one they hopped, crawled, skipped, and flew away.

Soon just the mouse, the frog, and the squirrel were left. They drifted off to sleep right there, all dreaming of one wish—to be bigger than the crocodile, bigger than the lion, bigger than the rhinoceros.

And when the sun rose over the Land of a Thousand Shadows, something strange had happened. The squirrel, the mouse, and the frog all woke up enormous. And they were all *enormously* happy.

Meanwhile the rhino, the lion, and the crocodile all woke up tiny. Bewildered, they stared at each other, then skulked away.

But soon the squirrel found out that being a giant wasn't easy. He was so heavy that branches broke under his weight. And he was so busy trying to find a few hundred pounds of acorns to eat that he had no time to worry about getting even with the rhinoceros. He missed being light as a feather, hopping from tree to tree with plenty of nuts to eat.

Not that the little rhinoceros had it any better. Now when he charged against a tree all he got was a head-ache. Yesterday everyone had been afraid of him, but today he was the one who was afraid. The rhinoceros was sorry he had been so nasty.

The giant mouse couldn't possibly fit in her old
burrow, and it was hard work digging a new one.
The mouse couldn't understand why she had wanted
to be bigger than the lion.

The lion was getting hungry, but he was much too
tiny to stalk his prey. "Must I be reduced to eating grass
like a donkey?" he grumbled, and thumped angrily
with his tail. But not a single blade of grass trembled.
The lion regretted his arrogant pride.

The giant frog sat in the tiny pond croaking
miserably. He'd spent the whole day catching flies, but
he could never catch enough to fill his great big belly.
The frog wished he'd never made his wish.

The little crocodile was so afraid he'd end up as fish
food that he didn't dare go near the water. And when
he heard the frog croaking, the crocodile trembled
to the tip of his tail, truly sorry that he'd ever been
so rude.

That night all the animals, big and small, had a meeting. Everyone agreed that things couldn't go on this way. They all promised to be good friends. The rhinoceros wouldn't knock down any more trees, the lion wouldn't roar so loudly, and the crocodile wouldn't gnash his teeth all the time.

And the next time the sun rose over the Land of a Thousand Shadows, the squirrel, the mouse, and the frog were small again, and the rhino, the lion, and the crocodile were large.

Pretty soon the lion happened to pass the little mouse. "Good morning," the lion greeted her warmly. "Is there anything I can do for you?"

"No, thank you, but it's nice of you to ask," the mouse squeaked back with a smile.

About the same time, the rhinoceros's head began to itch. He tramped gingerly over to the tree where the squirrel lived and said, "Excuse me, squirrel, may I please rub against your tree?"

All was friendly at the pond as well. "Hello, crocodile," croaked the frog. "I'm going out hopping in the meadow, so you go ahead and gnash your teeth if you want to."

And so the animals in the Land of a Thousand Shadows have lived in peace and friendship ever since.